GRETEL the WONDER MAMMOTH

Kim Hillyard

It was a perfectly peaceful Tuesday morning,
when suddenly, there was a loud

CRACK!

GRETEL

⟶

THE LAST MAMMOTH
ON EARTH

This Ladybird book belongs to

. . . .

For Astrid
K.H.

LADYBIRD BOOKS
Ladybird Books is part of the Penguin Random House group of companies
whose addresses can be found at global.penguinrandomhouse.com.
www.penguin.co.uk   www.puffin.co.uk   www.ladybird.co.uk

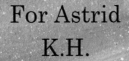

Penguin
Random House
UK

First published 2022
001
Text and illustrations copyright © Kim Hillyard, 2022
The moral right of the author/illustrator has been asserted
Printed in China

The authorized representative in the EEA is Penguin Random House Ireland,
Morrison Chambers, 32 Nassau Street, Dublin DO2 YH68

A CIP catalogue record for this book is available from the British Library
ISBN: 978–0–241–48856–0
All correspondence to:
Ladybird Books, Penguin Random House Children's
One Embassy Gardens, 8 Viaduct Gardens
London SW11 7BW

MIX
Paper from
responsible sources
FSC
www.fsc.org   FSC® C018179

Gretel had been asleep for

A VERY LONG TIME

so this was quite a surprise for everyone.

It was quite a surprise for Gretel, too.

INTRODUCING...
GRETEL
THE
WONDER
MAMMOTH!

Everyone loved Gretel.

She was gentle and kind.

She was strong and understanding.

And she told the best
bedtime stories.

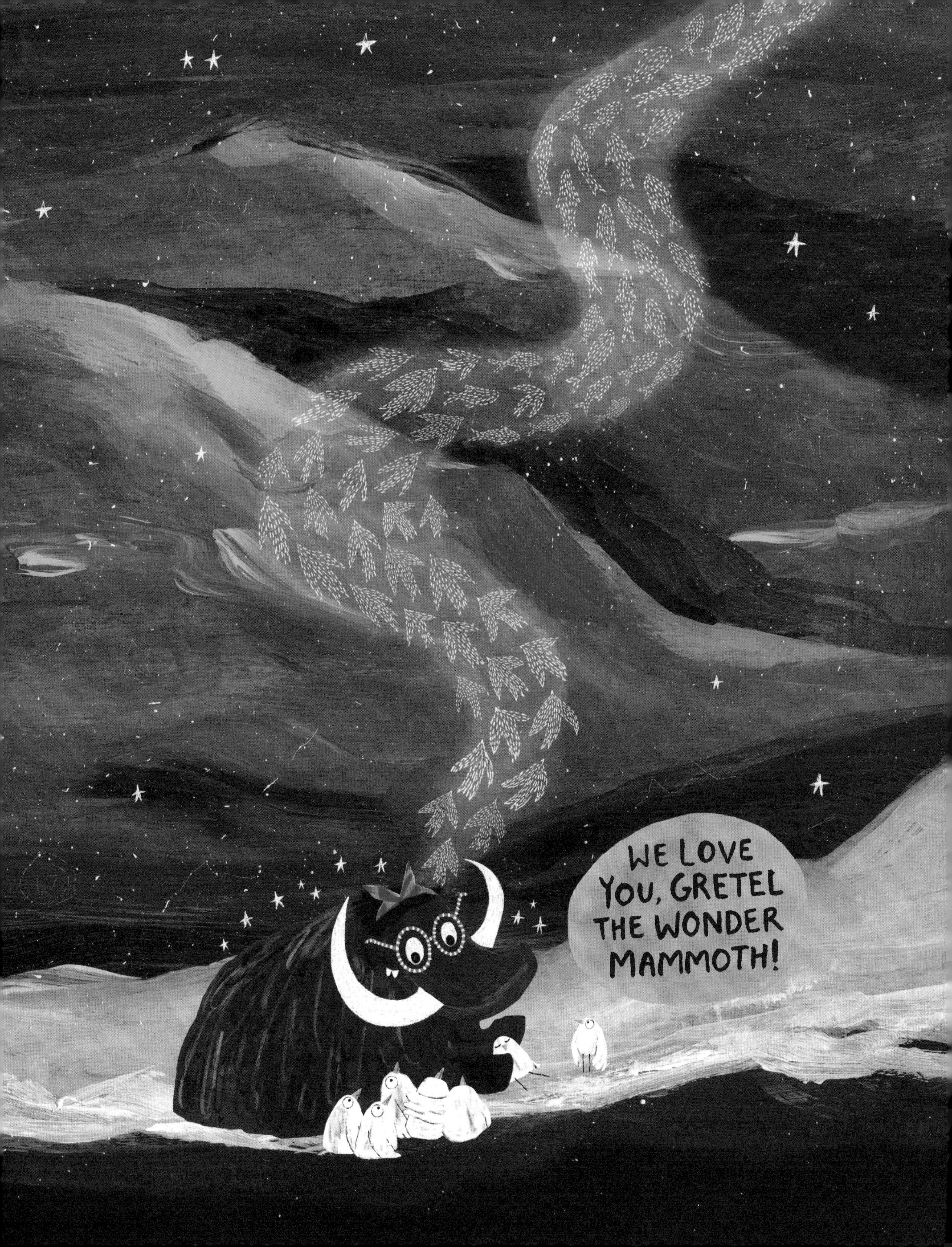
WE LOVE YOU, GRETEL THE WONDER MAMMOTH!

But Gretel did not feel like
a wonder mammoth.

The world she had woken up in was loud and confusing.
Some things moved very fast.

And some
didn't move
at all.

Gretel felt scared . . .

and sad . . .

and worried . . .

all at the same time.

She wanted to tell her friends how she was feeling . . .

but she didn't want to upset them.

So she decided to pretend that everything was fine.

WOW.

But it was
hard work.

Gretel just wanted
to be alone.

And at first this
made her feel better.

But soon it made her feel

MUCH WORSE.

It wasn't long before Gretel's friends came to find her.

And this is when Gretel did something very brave.

Gretel's friends listened to her very carefully.

They stroked her woolly feet,
and they helped her to feel less alone.

WE FOUND THIS.

THESE MAMMOTHS LOOK LIKE YOU!

WOW!

Gretel asked lots of questions,
and her friends tried their best to answer them.

Gretel soon found some new things
that made her feel good.

Gretel felt happy . . .

and excited . . .

and curious all at the same time. She felt like . . .

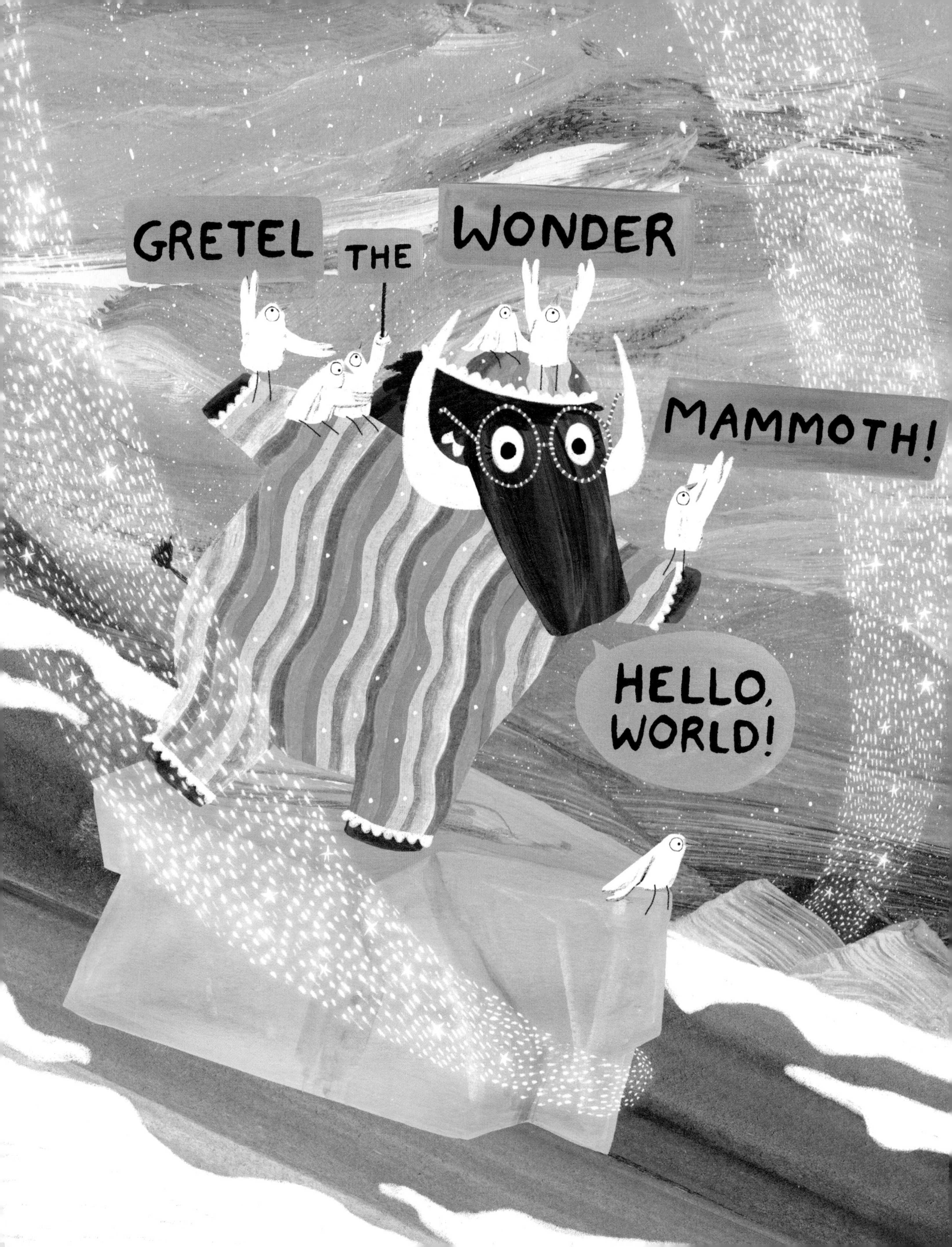
GRETEL
THE
WONDER
MAMMOTH!
HELLO, WORLD!